Lisa Olmstead would like to dedicate this book to her daughters Nicole and Korey. Without them, the book would have never been. Lisa would also like to dedicate it to her loving husband Steve, son Steven, daughter Kaitlin, and grandbabies Grayson, Scarlett, Sophia, Olivia, and Michael.

Nicole Diaz and Korey Olmstead would like to dedicate this book to their parents, wonderful kids, and loving husbands.

www.mascotbooks.com

Stinky Binky

©2017 Nicole Diaz, Lisa Olmstead, and Korey Olmstead. All Rights Reserved. No part of this publication may be reproduced, stored in a retrieval system or transmitted in any form by any means electronic, mechanical, or photocopying, recording or otherwise without the permission of the author.

For more information, please contact:
Mascot Books
560 Herndon Parkway #120
Herndon, VA 20170
info@mascotbooks.com

Library of Congress Control Number: 2017907709

CPSIA Code: PRT0917A
ISBN-13: 978-1-68401-314-2

Printed in the United States

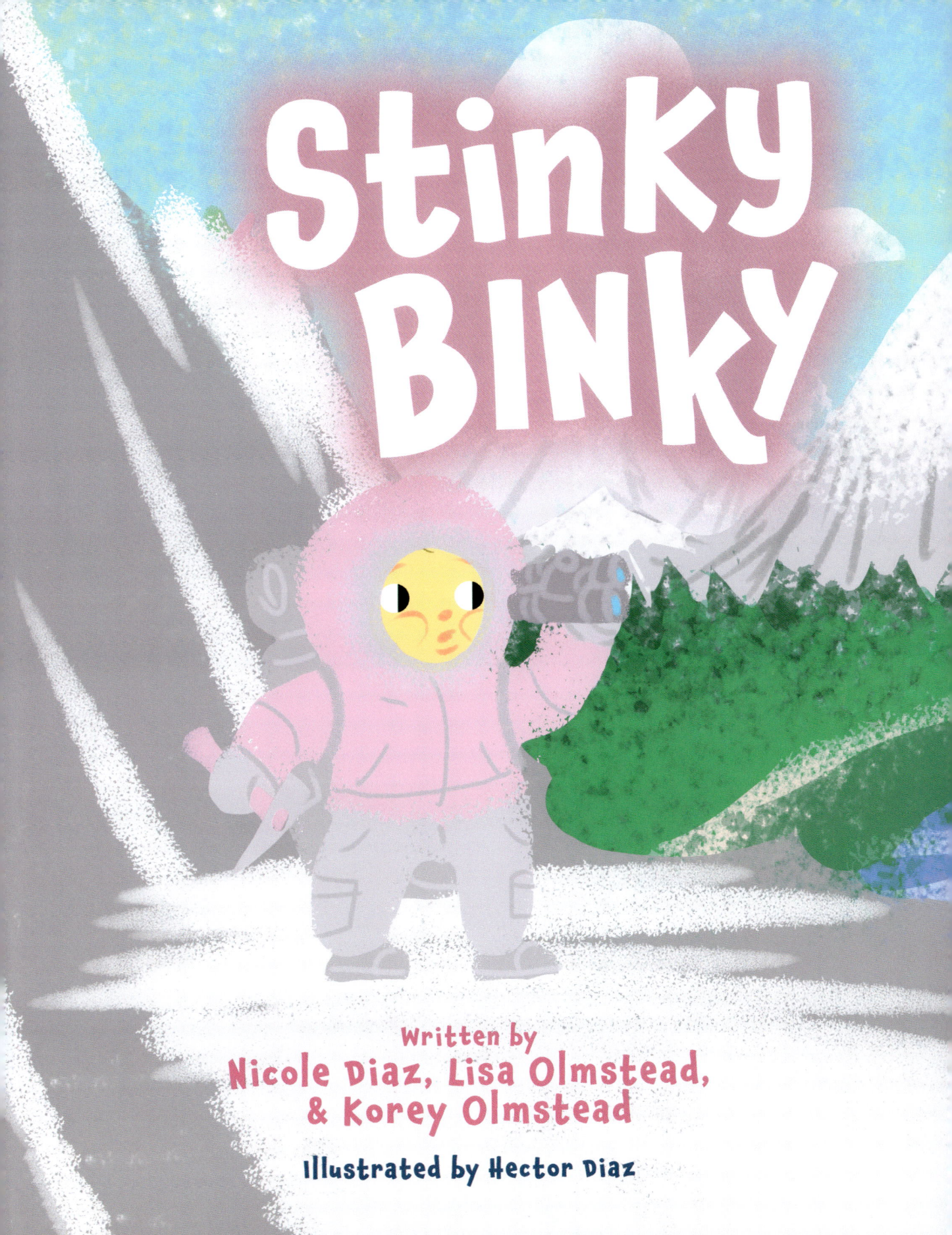

Scarlett Marie,
cute as can be,
loved her binky so!

Through day and night,
she held it tight
and never let it go!

Until one day, it disappeared
and Scarlett feared
she and Stinky Binky were no more!

She looked high!

She looked low!

Oh no!
It can't be so!
Where did Stinky Binky go?

"Oh my!"
Scarlett cried,
"Stinky Binky, is this goodbye?"

Looking every which way
with much dismay,
Scarlett searched from town to town.

But then, to her surprise,
no more tears filled her eyes
and a smile replaced her frown.

Without Stinky Binky's distraction,
Scarlett wishfully imagined
new adventures beyond her door.

From there she stood proud
and forever vowed,
"I will look for Stinky Binky no more!"

Scarlett Marie,
in her wondrous dreams,
started planning her next quest.

About the Authors

Stinky Binky was a collaboration between Lisa Olmstead and her daughters Nicole Diaz and Korey Olmstead. With the help of Nicole Diaz's brother-in-law Hector Diaz as the illustrator, it turned out to be a fun family project.

(Left) - Lisa Olmstead is the mother of four wonderful children and grandmother to five beautiful grandchildren. She resides with her loving husband of 30 years in Moyock, North Carolina. "It was such an enjoyment to work on this book with my daughters. I'm looking forward to future projects."

(Middle) - Korey Olmstead is the mother of an amazing little girl who was the inspiration for the book. She resides in Coinjock, North Carolina, with her wonderful fiancé.

(Right) - Nicole Diaz is the mother of an amazing little girl with a baby boy on the way. She resides in Elizabeth City, North Carolina, with her wonderful husband.

About the Illustrator

Hector Diaz is a talented artist from Nampa, Idaho. His work is versatile, ranging from paintings, ink drawings, ceramics, and cartoons just to name a few. This was his first children's book project and hopefully not his last. He lives with his partner Amanda, and together they are raising their wonderful kiddo Saul.